KAY THOMPSON'S ELO

Eloise and the
Very Secret Room

STORY BY **Ellen Weiss**

ILLUSTRATED BY **Tammie Lyon**

Ready-to-Read

Aladdin

NEW YORK · LONDON · TORONTO · SYDNEY

☛

ALADDIN PAPERBACKS
An imprint of Simon & Schuster Children's Publishing Division
1230 Avenue of the Americas, New York, NY 10020
Copyright © 2006 by the Estate of Kay Thompson
All rights reserved, including the right of
reproduction in whole or in part in any form.
"Eloise" and related marks are trademarks of the Estate of Kay Thompson.
READY-TO-READ is a registered trademark of Simon & Schuster, Inc.
ALADDIN PAPERBACKS and colophon are trademarks of
Simon & Schuster, Inc.
The text of this book was set in Century Old Style.
Manufactured in the United States of America
First Aladdin Paperbacks edition October 2006
2 4 6 8 10 9 7 5 3 1
Library of Congress Cataloging-in-Publication Data
Weiss, Ellen, 1949–
Eloise and the very secret room / story by Ellen Weiss ; illustrated by Tammie
Lyon.—1st Aladdin Paperbacks ed.
p. cm.— (Kay Thompson's Eloise) (Ready-to-read)
"Based on the art of Hilary Knight"—P. [1] of cover.
Summary: Eloise discovers the Plaza Hotel's Lost and Found
and decides to make it her secret playroom.
ISBN-13: 978-0-689-87450-5 (pbk)
ISBN-10: 0-689-87450-2 (pbk)
[1. Lost and found possessions—Fiction. 2. Plaza Hotel (New York, N.Y.)—Fiction.
3. Hotels, motels, etc.—Fiction. 4. Humorous stories.] I. Lyon, Tammie, ill.
II. Thompson, Kay, 1911– III. Knight, Hilary, ill. IV. Title. V. Series.
VI. Series: Ready-to-read.
PZ7.W4475Elo 2006
[E]—dc22
2005029648

My name is Eloise.
I am six.

I live on
the tippy-top floor
of The Plaza Hotel.

But I can go all over.

This is Skipperdee.
He wears sneakers.
Sometimes.

Skipperdee and I
like to take walks.

Here is what I like to do:
go down
that very, very,
long, long hall.

(It is the one that
goes past the room
with the stringy mops.)

There is a room
that is so secret
only I know about it.

Skipperdee and I, anyway.

It says LOST AND FOUND.

Maybe it is lost,
but I found it.

There are very good things in it.

If you tie a lot of
ties together,
you can jump rope.

It is also a good room
to spin in.

If we get tired,
we take a nap on a
fur coat.

Here is what else I can do:
wear nineteen hats.

A tennis racket makes
a very good turtle carrier.

I do not think anyone
has ever been in
this room but me.

It is a good room
to practice hollering in.

A hatbox makes a very good drum.

In comes Nanny.
"Eloise!" she says.
"Here you are!"

In comes the manager.
"Eloise!" he says.
"Here you are!"

"Of course I am here,"
I say.
"Where else would I be?"

"We found you
   in the Lost and Found,"
says Nanny.

I was not lost at all.
I was right here
all the time.
Oooooooo I love, love, love
the Lost and Found.

Tomorrow I will see if that hat makes a good fishbowl.